I0783528

below
existence

esther graham

RABBIT HOUSE PRESS

Versailles, KY 40383

For inquiries about author appearances and/or volume orders contact us at rabbithousepress.com.

ISBN: 979-8-9907833-9-3

Edited by Erin Chandler

Cover and interior design; formatting: Brooke Lee

Photographs by Esther Graham

below existence

esther graham

RABBIT
HOUSE
PRESS

rabbithousepress.com

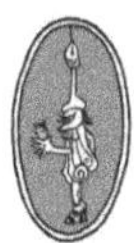

*have you ever left a conversation and when time
passed on you finally found the right words to say?*

*dedicated to the ones who find writing what you want
to say easier than actually saying it.*

invasive; evasive

it's ironic
how my brain, so hidden, too covered to assume its size
could do so much damage to a girl like me
more even with contents immeasurable
we can switch places
i'll hide
it can experience what being controlled feels like

notice

i notice i write in paste tense
as if i'm recovered, cured, maybe even dead

it never crossed my mind
coming out naturally

perhaps subconsciously, i was having trouble
accepting my issues
i was always afraid
timely wanting attention
infatuated
stalkerish
relying on medications i couldn't even pronounce
a misanthrope

so, it appeared on the paper

i was aware of who i was
though i didn't feel it in a way to where it hit me in the face
while having trouble obtaining it

in consciousness, fixing these mistakes
anticipating the day

i'd see i am the invisible, seen between the lines of the writing

poisonous

the world is toxic
some are just more prone to its poison

describe yourself

it all came to the disorder,
you are your symptoms

i recognize myself as i read the list(s)
irritable
depressed
anxious
impulsive
hyperactive
absent-minded
forgetful
socially isolated
distorted self-image
frequent mood-swings

do i even have a personality?
am i the chemical imbalance that stole who i was to
become?

some get to be their true selves
while i pretend

waiting for it to someday
come naturally

disappear into thin air
maybe go bother someone else who deserves it

take a few years off
someone else's life

feel it all

i was never able to listen to sad music
now i welcome it in
letting the lyrics flow through my body
like medication
allowing the sound to make me contemplate,
dread the wrong
fixed in a crowded room
gazing at what i'm missing
what it could be; what i maladapted
pained by the hopelessness
though acceptant
i allow it to take over

different

the thing about hopelessness is it doesn't actually disappear
unknowingly, you learn to live with it
on days of my acceptance
days where i admire everything
dead or alive
even in object form
for just being there
days where i smiled
thinking about all the little things going right in my life
how it fit perfectly
like there was an imaginary puzzle inside my head
when i finish a school paper
rest my hand
i won't be writing that ever again
complacent but at peace
then it crept back
i can't say how many times it happened
what day it was
but i knew the feeling
i had no power but to sit in bed imagining the courage
it would take to act on these thoughts
i try to think about good things again
build a puzzle once more
get the strength to get out of bed
i didn't care
it didn't give me butterflies in my stomach
or the feeling of wanting to jump up and down
i didn't care at all

the pit in my stomach when i felt like everything
was going to be okay
wasn't there
i felt hopeless
i felt different

eviction

depression is the tenant of the mind

five years ago, it rented out empty space inside my head
gradually, it began to spread and occupy everything else
until the only thing left
was depression

i tried evicting depression
giving a week notice
i needed it out by the new year
to never step onto my property again

still, wouldn't leave
hopeless i felt
i started to believe the only way to get rid of it
was to demolish the house

to my last resort

to my last resort
please do not leave
no one else will listen without interrupting
like how the moon interferes with the sun

but do not judge me for being insane and full of hatred
i will never laugh at the way you quickly lose your ink then
become useless
i will never get mad because when someone isn't careful
enough
you will rip into worthlessness

that's just how you're made
this is how i'm made
i will be careful with your flaws
if you are careful with mine

misunderstood

i'm not a bad person
just perpetually defined by my bad days

below existence

suicide can't answer your questions
or fix your issues
it will only keep them lingering

if you are dead, you don't know
you can't be there to get your answer
lifelessness has no life

no existence

promise

i don't get how people are so happy
when the only thing promised is death

the trance

while in depression's trance
i have to deal with it, to live
accept the things i do
when released from this state of mind
i can get out
accept and understand who i am
that's why i am here now

buttons

so many buttons
unseen
small
open for the asking

you never know until
unknowingly pushed
worst fears come true
life becomes a joke

surrounded by overthinking
until your brain shuts down
as you sleep
temporary time

life
for some reason
doesn't given warnings
chance to show control

people ask
why are you paranoid
why are you slurring over words
why name the impossible

i'll never know
will it come back for more
shed me down
from skin to bones

not built for this world
something pierces into me
invisible
i wait for it to creep back

circle of life

the bird fell from its nest
the deer ran across the road
the dog escaped the fence
the spider found its way inside a house
the cat passed its limit
the mouse couldn't outrun the seeker

that's what people call the circle of life

solitude

when i'm free, know where to find me

i'll be walking around endless fields on gray days
i'll be picking oranges and lemons
i'll be walking around bookstores, coffee in hand
i'll be buying flowers from nurseries on rainy days
i'll be walking along the beach during sunsets
i'll be swinging on a tree swing, music in my ears
i'll be baking pastries in my kitchen at dawn
in front of a window where dim lights reflect
i'll be writing next to a lit candle
letting the smell of peace travel
i'll be watering my perennial flowers
welcoming them back home
i'll then go to sleep
and dream not of a life where it was peaceful and perfect
because my life is already that

there's a flower dying in my closet

there's a flower dying in my closet
i feed it old water
only when i remember
then shut it into dark
behind two sliding doors
neglecting it from light
still
it grows
amongst pots i emptied
ones who withered away
there's a flower dying in my closet

leaves are still growing

house on the hill

it was nighttime
i left my house inching forward
taking a breath
closing my eyes
then seeing again
it was quiet
nothing disturbed
wind conversed with the trees
dashing here and there
free it sounded
vivacious it seemed
though disquieted was i
it was deceitful
they were laughing at me
i opened my eyes

the journey to unnatural happiness

first a lingering feeling sinks deeper
deeper into your stomach
every thought morphed into an idea
until it's there for good
uncontrollable

unless it's a dream
not part of life
morning comes and i pretend
but the pit in my stomach says otherwise

life behind eyes indulged in the promise
tomorrow will continue
has now faded
fully formed, not a state of mind
but a step into the real world
the world you're not told exists

you discover its flaws while hanging by a thread
the hole has spread and guts are still there to speak up
there's another step
silicone sheets
synchronized silverware
an old telephone
uncomfortable talks
doors that never close
no matter how long they stay on the hinges
only sense of stability
are the grips beneath your feet

this place your issues are seen as power
is it just ideation
or abandonment
the memory strikes
and a new definition of happiness
is if time beyond yesterday
doesn't set off lingering pain of wasted life

to and from

it wasn't my birthday
but a knock wounded the door

a present laid there
with deriving eyes
a naive bow
covered in crisp, burning paper

no indication
an unnerving word followed

fruit man

everyone is happy
so is the sun
the grill let out smoke
so hot you could feel it
from miles away
i smile
wearing my oversized shirt
that protects my legs
from bugs

a sharp pain surrounds my head
though my hair is clean
my outfit matches the occasion
for once

same morning
warped eyelids
waking to a surreal dream
where my fear was under the bed
it's almost nostalgic
distasteful

eight days since the hysteric incident
where burning internal pain left scars
permanently

as i stay outside
on the tree
swinging
gossiping

night hit again
permanently, inside
i ignite

loneliness

i am a tree
i live in a field of other trees
though i stand alone
distant from others

glancing around,
i glimpse the familiar
altered leaves
cylinder trunks bending side to side
holding on for dear life

i was the same
i had leaves and a branch
though no trees grew around me
or fell down to my feet

spring ends and summer begins

remember how our arms so calmly touched
i'm reminded I felt that force
you not at all
remember that gaze
i'm reminded it never occurred
my head never turned
as spring ends and summer begins
i'm reminded
that was a version of you only inside my head

**your *story* shouldn't matter to those who don't
want to pick up your book**

spending too much time
convincing your state of mind
wastes time

the only person interested in getting to know me
will black out
any second now

and just in case the schizophrenic's reality
was contagious
i kept my mouth closed

although the orphaned girl was down-and-out
she held superiority
no one told her
that's inferiority

face it
the body can't handle such force
the paranoid is dead
persistent setback is still setback

the staff got new jobs
ones they actually like
not for money or convenience

away i go
my brain is not incapable
or filled with conceptual terror
on the verge of collapse

my map expanded
that's not selfish

on the sea

i found myself on the beach
wishing it was just me on the sand
with the ocean

the ocean has been there for centuries
living, dead, the two become
it doesn't talk
doesn't pretend to be something it isn't
it is a body of water
and that is it

sometimes we can tell what it has to say
when there is a natural disaster
it's angry
during regular days
it's calm
bringing seashells to the shore

once you're there
it is real
peaceful
it feels like a cure

with each movement it takes your thoughts
and swallows them

i believe the only way
this ocean could disappear
is if gravity stops
and the sea falls off earth

don't tell me that's not scientific
or true
that's how i see it
the ocean stays itself
until the worst possible thing happens

gravity is the only thing that can stop the ocean
gravity should be the only thing that can stop the
ocean

what am i?

i've been a tablet
i've been a capsule
i've been oval shaped
i've been circle shaped
i've been green
i've been blue

i've been to 5
up to 10
then up to 15
down to 10
then up to 20

i've dissolved quickly
i've fallen out of a hand

though i've never been a star

who am i?

observations

pieces of hair hang along the curtain rod
in front of the oddly carved door
and its water-stained brass handle

the trash overflows with a women's despair
along the uneven paint
down to the wall trim

i look to my feet
swollen from trapped steam
drowning from escaped water

i wait till the vertigo goes away

parallel world

parallel lines never meet
like the parallel world inside my head

in one world
i'm an actress
a screenwriter
director

surreal lighting, haze

i write
words come naturally
truth never dies

in the other
i carry no confidence to be an actress
but i'd love to play a role
embrace my dull blonde hair

screenplays are stored inside my head
as i struggle to grasp scenes
words never match the situation

parallel lines never meet
like the parallel world inside my head

philosophy

we live in a philosophy, a philosophical earth

nothing about existence
will truly be answered
knowledge is limited
reason is like a light switch
and value expires

beliefs linger
suddenly dissolve

we live once
never knowing why